EDDIE *and* LOUELLA

By the Same Author

Published by William Morrow and Company

SNOWBOUND WITH BETSY. 1962
ANNIE PAT AND EDDIE. 1960
EDDIE AND LOUELLA. 1959
BETSY'S WINTERHOUSE. 1958
EDDIE MAKES MUSIC. 1957
BETSY'S BUSY SUMMER. 1956
EDDIE AND HIS BIG DEALS. 1955
BETSY AND THE CIRCUS. 1954
EDDIE'S PAY DIRT. 1953
THE MIXED-UP TWINS. 1952
EDDIE AND GARDENIA. 1951
BETSY'S LITTLE STAR. 1950
EDDIE AND THE FIRE ENGINE. 1949
PENNY GOES TO CAMP. 1948
LITTLE EDDIE. 1947

Published by Harcourt, Brace and World

PENNY AND PETER. 1946
BETSY AND THE BOYS. 1945
HERE'S A PENNY. 1944
BACK TO SCHOOL WITH BETSY. 1943
PRIMROSE DAY. 1942
BETSY AND BILLY. 1941
TWO AND TWO ARE FOUR. 1940
"B" IS FOR BETSY. 1939

EDDIE
and LOUELLA

Written and Illustrated by

CAROLYN HAYWOOD

New York, 1959
WILLIAM MORROW & COMPANY

Fourth Printing, September, 1963

Library of Congress Catalog Card Number 59–10547

TO
Caroline R. McDougal,
my California pen pal since she was four.

CONTENTS

1   Louella Goes Round and Round   13

2   A Lot of Funny Business   31

3   The Dog and Mr. Wilson   47

4   Eddie Goes for His Parrot   64

5   Eddie Tells the News   83

6   Louella Takes a Ride   101

7   The Special Delivery Letter   121

8   Eddie, the Human Sandwich   137

9   The Famous Eddie   157

10   Straightened Out at Last   176

EDDIE *and* LOUELLA

CHAPTER 1

LOUELLA GOES ROUND AND ROUND

Eddie Wilson considered his collection of valuable property the very finest in the neighborhood. While it was true that his friend Sidney Stewart, who lived next door, had many things that Eddie admired, he looked upon most of her collection as junk. As for his friend Anna Patricia and the stuff she called her things, Eddie scorned the whole lot; for Anna Patricia collected dolls, and dolls, to Eddie, were not valuable property.

Sidney at least had some live things, like the two poodles and the guppies. But the poodles were sort of silly, with their pink and blue hair ribbons, and after you had filled up every jar in the house with guppies, what did you have? Just more guppies, all exactly alike.

Eddie liked variety. "Guppies," he said to Sidney, "are only good for trading." He had traded his last jar of guppies for a bag of confetti. He liked the bright-colored bits of paper. They were good for sprinkling in Anna Patricia's curls.

Anna Patricia hated confetti in her hair. She had to brush and brush to get it out.

"You should thank me," said Eddie. "Makes muscle."

"Mind your own muscles," Anna Patricia replied.

Eddie had had various animals ever since he was old

enough to walk around the block. He was always bringing home stray dogs and cats. Rewards for finding other people's dogs had added greatly to the weight of Eddie's bank. Lost dogs seemed to find Eddie, instead of Eddie's finding the lost dogs. He drew them to him like a magnet. The result was that Eddie's pets were always changing—all except Louella.

Louella was Eddie's parrot. He had brought Louella back from Texas when he visited his Uncle Ed and Aunt Minnie.

Eddie loved Louella and Louella loved Eddie, but she was jealous. She was jealous of all stray animals and she called them all cats. When Eddie came into the house with a bedraggled dog, Louella would scream, "Cats! Cats!"

Even the birds that came to the bird feeder outside the window were cats to Louella. She would squawk and scold and then say, "Cats!"

15

Cats themselves, she despised. If a cat appeared in the room, she closed her eyes and made believe it wasn't there. Every once in a while she would open one eye. If the cat was still in sight she would ruffle up her feathers and pretend to be asleep.

When Eddie brought Louella from Texas, she had said one thing over and over—"Texas is better!" Eddie soon changed that. He taught her to say, "Eddie is best." This made his brothers, Rudy, and Joe and Frank, the twins, very mad and they called Louella that dumb bird!

But Louella was not dumb. She just made mistakes sometimes; as she did when she called Mrs. Wilson's new furniture junk. Afterwards, Eddie taught Louella to call his mother Pretty Girl, and Mrs. Wilson and Louella were friends again.

One afternoon when Eddie came home from school, his mother said to him, "Eddie, the committee that is planning the big dance to raise money for the Old Ladies' Home would like to borrow Louella."

"What do they want with Louella?" said Eddie. "She can't dance."

"They want to use her in the decorations," said his mother.

"In the decorations!" exclaimed Eddie. "Like a Christmas-tree ornament?"

His mother laughed. "Not exactly," she said. "You see, the ball is a tropical ball and the decorations are going to be palm trees, so the committee thought it would be nice to borrow some parrots."

"They won't let Louella out of her cage, will they?" said Eddie. "I might never get her back."

"Oh, no!" his mother replied. "They are going to hang the cages in the ballroom. Louella will be all right. Don't worry."

"Well, if you think she will be all right, they can have

her," said Eddie. Then he laughed and said, "I'll bet Louella never expected to go to a ball. I hope she doesn't squawk too much."

Mrs. Wilson laughed. "If she squawks, everyone will know she is a live parrot, not a stuffed one."

"How many parrots do you think they will have?" Eddie asked.

"I haven't any idea," replied his mother. "They had it written up in the paper. They want to get as many as possible."

"When is the ball?" asked Eddie.

"Next Friday evening," said his mother. "They want Louella in the afternoon."

"Where is this ball?" Eddie asked.

"In the ballroom of the hotel," said Mrs. Wilson. "We'll drive down with Louella about four o'clock."

On Friday afternoon Eddie cleaned Louella's cage. "Listen, old girl," he said, "you're going to a ball."

18

"Yawk!" said Louella. "What's cookin'!"

"See that you behave yourself," said Eddie. "No funny business."

"Yawk! No funny business!" said Louella. "Junk!"

"No it isn't junk," said Eddie. "It's a swell ball."

"Yawk!" said Louella. "Eddie is best."

Eddie laughed. "Maybe you won't think so when you see all those people at that ball. They'll all be dressed up like pirates, I guess."

At half past four the Wilson car drew up at the door of the hotel. Eddie was sitting beside his mother on the front seat, with Louella's cage between them.

"I'll wait right here," said Eddie's mother. "You take Louella in."

"Where do I take her?" Eddie asked.

"Ask at the desk," said his mother.

"O.K.!" said Eddie, as he opened the door of the car. He lifted the cage off the front seat.

As Eddie carried Louella to the door of the hotel, a dog rushed up to Eddie, barking. He was barking at Louella.

"Yawk!" cried Louella. "Cats!"

The dog jumped at the cage. Eddie lifted the cage higher. "Go away!" he said to the dog. "Beat it!"

The hotel had a revolving door. Eddie stepped in. The dog kept on jumping.

"Down!" said Eddie. "Go 'way!"

The dog pushed in with Eddie.

Eddie lifted the cage and held it in front of him. There was a brass rod on the door to push against. Eddie pushed. The door revolved and in a moment it was time to step out into the hotel, but the dog was in the way. Someone was pushing from behind, so Eddie and the parrot and the dog went around again. When they reached the outside, Eddie said, "Get out, dog! Get out." The dog stayed. He liked Eddie very well by this time.

"Cats! Cats!" cried Louella.

"Bow-wow-wow-wow," barked the dog.

"Mother!" Eddie yelled.

His mother jumped out of the car, but before she reached the door a man wanted to go into the hotel. Eddie and Louella and the dog started around again.

When they reached the inside of the hotel, the doorman was there. "Take that dog out," he said. "No dogs allowed in this hotel." The doorman gave the door a push, and Eddie and the parrot and the dog were again on their way out.

When they reached the outside, Eddie's mother was waiting. "Mother!" said Eddie. "I can't get rid of this dog."

Eddie's mother called to the dog. "Here, boy!" she said. "Come along!"

The dog sat down beside Eddie.

"Come, boy!" said his mother.

A man carrying a suitcase came along. "I'm sorry," he said. "I should like to go into the hotel."

Eddie pushed the door. The dog got up, the man stepped in behind Eddie, and they were off again.

Inside, the doorman said, "I told you to take that dog out. Now don't try to bring him in again."

"I'm not bringing him in," said Eddie. "I'm bringing Louella." That was as far as Eddie got. There was a push from behind, and around he went again.

Outside, he said, "Here, Mother, you take Louella and I'll stay outside with the dog." Eddie tried to hand the cage to his mother, but he discovered that the cage was caught in the brass rod fastened to the door. He pulled at it, trying to shake it loose.

"Yawk!" cried Louella. "What's cookin'!"

Eddie's mother stepped inside the door to see if she could unfasten the cage.

"I beg your pardon," said a lady's voice. "I should like to go into the hotel."

"Oh, excuse me!" said Mrs. Wilson, stepping out.

25

Once again Eddie and Louella and the dog went around. When the doorman saw them for the third time, he said, "If you bring that dog in here again, I'll call the police."

"I don't want to bring the dog in," said Eddie. "I want to bring my parrot in."

"Well, then, give me the parrot!" said the doorman.

"I can't," said Eddie, but before he could say why, there was a push from behind and out went Eddie and the parrot and the dog once more.

Outside, his mother said, "Get out, Eddie. Get out and the dog will follow you. I'll see if I can get the cage unhooked."

Eddie stepped out and sure enough, the dog went with him.

Before his mother could step in, someone who was leaving the hotel pushed from inside and Louella went around by herself, securely hooked to the door.

26

When the doorman saw the parrot all by herself he was surprised. He stepped in and tried to lift the cage out.

"Yawk! No funny business!" cried Louella.

Once again the door was pushed, and now it was the doorman who went around with Louella. Outside, he said to Mrs. Wilson, "What's this all about?"

"My son is trying to deliver his parrot for the ball," said Mrs. Wilson. "The cage is caught on the bar."

"So I see!" said the doorman. "I'll see if I can get it off."

"No funny business!" Louella called out.

Eddie, with the dog close beside him, watched the doorman.

"That dog has been around here for two days," said the doorman. "Is he your dog?"

"No, he's not mine," said Eddie. "But he's a nice dog," he added, patting the dog on the head.

"He's a nuisance!" said the doorman.

"Cats!" said Louella.

Suddenly the cage came unhooked. "There!" said the doorman. "I'll take this parrot in and deliver it to the right place."

"Thanks a lot," said Eddie. "Her name is Louella. Take good care of her, won't you?"

"Don't worry about her," said the doorman.

"My name and address are on the tag," said Eddie. "It's fastened to the cage. She has plenty of food in her cage, but maybe you'd better give her more water. Just in case it spilled out."

"O.K.!" said the doorman. "Don't worry. She'll be all right."

Eddie followed his mother to the car. The dog followed Eddie. "This poor dog!" said Eddie, in a very doleful voice. "Just think! He has been here for two days. Poor thing! No food! All alone!"

"Now, Eddie!" said his mother. "Your father has said, 'No dogs!' "

"But he's my friend," said Eddie.

"Your friend!" exclaimed his mother. "When did he become your friend?"

"Why on all those trips we had together, going round and round," said Eddie. "He's a nice dog. He looks like a golden retriever."

"He doesn't have a collar or tag," said his mother.

"Maybe he lost it," said Eddie. "If we don't take him, somebody will telephone to the dogcatchers and they will take him to the shelter. He's an awful nice dog!"

"Get in," said his mother. "Put the dog in the back."

Eddie's face was wreathed in smiles. "I'll look in the paper in the 'Lost and Found' part. Maybe I can find the owner."

"Maybe," said his mother.

Eddie turned and looked back at the dog. This was

the nicest dog Eddie had ever found. "Mother," said Eddie, "do I have to look hard or can I just look a little bit?"

"Eddie," said his mother, "you are the limit!"

CHAPTER 2

A LOT OF FUNNY BUSINESS

THE doorman handed the cage with Louella in it to a bellboy. "Here, Willie," he said. "Take this parrot up to the fifth floor."

"O.K.!" said Willie.

When he stepped into the elevator, the operator said, "Another parrot, hey?"

"That's right!" said Willie. "This makes nine. I didn't know there were so many parrots in this town."

"How do you keep from getting them mixed up?" the elevator boy asked. "They all look alike to me."

"Oh, they all have tags on their cages," said Willie. He picked up the tag and read it. "This one belongs to Edward Wilson."

"They're supposed to talk," said the elevator boy, "but I never heard one say anything."

"Yawk!" said Louella.

"What did I tell you!" said the elevator boy, as he opened the door at the fifth floor.

"The last one I brought up said 'Nuts!' " said Willie, as he stepped off.

When Willie carried Louella into the cloakroom, Louella looked at the other parrots and shouted, "Cats!"

When all the parrots had been delivered to the hotel,

there were eleven. Their cages were lined up on a table. They were all squawking like a chorus.

"It sounds like the birdhouse at the zoo, doesn't it, Pete?" said Willie to the bellboy in charge of the parrots.

"They make a racket," said Pete.

"The manager says we're to put them in the ballroom now," said Willie.

"Where do we put 'em?" asked Pete.

"Boss says to put 'em on the big chandeliers," Willie replied.

Pete looked at the parrots. "Some of these birds look an awful lot alike," he said. "Fellow would have to be real smart to tell 'em apart."

Willie looked them over. "That's right," he said.

"Are these birds smart?" asked Pete.

"Sure they're smart," said Willie. "I'll bet these parrots understand everything you say to 'em."

"Do you mean it?" said Pete.

"That's what I've been told," said Willie. Willie looked at his watch. "Seven o'clock," he said. "I have to carry some bags down for a man in 318. You get started with the parrots."

Willie went off and Pete was left alone with the parrots. He picked up one cage in each hand and carried the cages into the ballroom. There was no one in the ballroom when Pete walked in. He looked around the room and thought the decorations were beautiful. He walked to the center of the room and looked up at a big chandelier. "Now, look, you birds!" he said to the parrots. "You're to sit up on that chandelier."

"Yawk! Yawk!" said the two parrots.

"No foolin'," said Pete, opening the door of one of the cages.

"Yawk!" said the parrots.

"Come on! Out with you," said Pete.

34

The parrot jumped off its perch. Then, in a moment, it stepped outside its cage.

"Hurry up!" said Pete. "Right up there," he said, pointing above him.

The parrot flew, but not up to the chandelier. It flew to a curtain pole and sat down.

"You dumb cluck!" said Pete. "I thought you were supposed to be smart." The parrot just sat and looked around.

"Here!" said Pete, opening the door of the other cage. "You show that dummy what he is supposed to do."

The second bird left its cage as soon as the door was opened, but this one flew into a palm tree.

"You're just as dumb as the other one," said Pete. "Over here! Over here!" he called out, pointing to the chandelier.

Just then the door opened and Willie came in, with

a cage in each hand. He was surprised to find Pete running around the room, waving his arms, and shouting, "Over here! Over here!"

"Hey! What's up!" Willie called.

"Those dumb birds won't get on that chandelier," Pete called back.

Willie set his cages down. "You don't mean you let the parrots out of their cages!" he cried.

"You told me to put them on the chandelier," said Pete.

"Not the birds," cried Willie. "The cages. The cages are supposed to hang on the chandeliers. "You're dumber than the parrots. If the boss finds out, you'll be fired for this."

"Well, help me get them back in the cages," said Pete.

"I don't know how to get them back in their cages," said Willie.

"Parrots like crackers, don't they?" said Pete. "I'll

get some crackers." Pete dashed out of the room for crackers.

While he was gone, Willie hung the rest of the cages on the chandeliers.

When the parrots in the cages saw the other two parrots flying from tree to tree and from curtain poles to window sills, they set up a terrible chatter. They all wanted to be outside.

Before long Pete was back, with a paper bag in his hand. "I got all the different kinds of crackers they had down in the kitchen," he said. "There should be some cracker here that they like." Pete opened the bag and pulled out a handful of crackers. He held one up. "Polly want a cracker?" he called. "Polly want a cracker?"

To Pete's surprise the whole chandelier began to chatter, "Polly wants a cracker."

The two free parrots flew around the room. Pete ran after them holding up first one cracker and then another. "Polly want a cracker?" he called. "See—all kinds of crackers."

"Put the crackers in the cages," said Willie. "Do you think those birds are going to come down and sit on your finger?"

"O.K.!" said Pete.

The two empty cages were sitting side by side on a bench. "Look!" said Pete, to the two parrots. "Crackers!" He put some crackers in each cage.

In a few moments one of the parrots flew down and perched on top of one of the empty cages. Pete held his breath. So did Willie. "If those birds don't get back in those cages before the ball begins, you are as good as a dead duck," Willie said to Pete.

"They'll get back," said Pete. "They have to get back. They just have to."

"I wish they would make up their minds," said Willie.

The parrot on top of the cage hopped down to the

bench. It poked its head through the door. Both Pete and Willie were afraid to breathe. Just as Pete and Willie were about to burst, the parrot stepped inside. Pete quickly closed the door.

"Well, that's one back, anyway," he said.

The boys looked around for the other parrot. It was sitting on one of the big fronds of a palm tree.

"Come on, Polly," Pete coaxed. "Polly want a cracker?"

"Sure! Polly's crazy for a cracker," Willie sneered.

Pete carried the cage over to a tree and hung it nearby on a wall bracket.

The parrot immediately took off for a curtain pole.

Pete unhooked the cage and carried it to the window sill.

The parrot flew to a chandelier, which threw the rest of the parrots into a frenzy. "Yawk! Yawk!" they screamed. They seemed to be cheering for the bird.

43

"Pete, stop running around," said Willie. "That bird will never go into its cage with you running after it."

Pete put the cage back on the bench. "O.K.!" he said. "Let's make believe we don't care." Pete walked to the window and looked out.

Willie joined him. "Say, Pete!" he said. "Suppose the wrong birds get into those cages. Have you thought of that?"

"Oh, they wouldn't get into the wrong cages," said Pete. "They're smart enough to know their own cage. You don't get into the wrong house when you go home, do you?"

"No," said Willie, "but I'm not a parrot."

"Even if they did," said Pete, "they look exactly alike. Nobody could ever tell the difference."

"Well, I just hope that bird over there is the bird that belongs in that cage," said Willie.

The boys turned from the window and looked at the two cages on the bench.

"Oh!" cried Pete. "They're both in!"

Pete dashed to the bench and closed the door of the cage.

"Look at those two birds," he said to Willie. "They look like twins. Nobody could tell them apart."

"Wonder who they belong to?" said Willie. He picked up the tag fastened to the first cage. "The name on it is Tomkins," he said.

The parrot inside ruffled up its feathers and said, "Hello, Pretty Girl!"

"Ho, ho!" laughed Pete. "Did you hear what that bird called you? It called you Pretty Girl!"

"I heard it," said Willie.

"Who owns the other one?" Pete asked.

Willie read the tag. "This one belongs to Edward Wilson," he said. The parrot inside yelled, "Old Sourpuss!"

"Say, Willie!" said Pete. "These parrots can sure enough talk."

45

"Yeah!" said Willie. "And have you thought what that means? It means trouble ahead if they are mixed up."

"Oh, any bird that is smart enough to talk is smart enough to get into its right cage," said Pete.

"Time will tell!" said Willie. "Time will tell!"

CHAPTER 3

THE DOG AND MR. WILSON

WHEN Eddie arrived home with the dog his brothers were delighted. "This time you've brought home a real dog," said his oldest brother, Rudy.

"He sure did!" said Joe. "Cleaned up, he would be a beaut."

"Mother says I have to find its owner," said Eddie, in a sad tone of voice.

"I think anybody who owns a dog like that and doesn't keep a collar on him doesn't deserve to get their dog back," said Frank.

"That's what I think," said Eddie.

"But Dad said the next dog you brought home would have to go straight to the shelter," said Rudy.

Eddie's face grew longer. "Oh, but not a nice dog like this!" said Eddie.

Eddie's mother called from the dining room. "I reminded you, Eddie, when we picked up the dog, that your father said there were to be no more stray dogs."

"You'd better call him up at the office right now," said Frank. "Because if he walks in and sees that dog he won't like it. Maybe if you talk to him before he sees it, he will say O.K."

"I guess that's a good idea," said Eddie.

Eddie went to the telephone and dialed his father's office number. "Dad!" said Eddie, when his father said hello. "I have a wonderful surprise for you!"

"You have!" said his father. "I know your surprises, Eddie. What have you brought home now?"

"Oh, Dad! You'll be crazy about him," said Eddie.

"Oh! So it's a 'him,' is it?" said his father. "What kind of a him? Not a dog!"

"Well . . . er," Eddie stammered, "a sort of a dog."

"A sort of!" said his father. "I never heard of a sort of a dog. Either it's a dog or it isn't a dog. Now Edward! Is it a dog?"

His father was calling him Edward. This was bad.

Eddie cleared his throat, and in a very small voice he said, "It's a dog."

"Now Edward!" said his father. "You know I told you that I wanted no more dirty stray mutts brought into the house."

Eddie wished his father wouldn't keep calling him Edward.

"But, Dad!" he said. "This one isn't a mutt. Mother and I think he's a golden retriever. Maybe I'll get a reward for finding him. Mother let him sit on the back seat of the car."

"Your mother is too soft," said his father, "but I am going to take that animal to the shelter this very evening. He is not going to spend one night in the house. I am tired of running a boardinghouse for strays."

"O.K.!" said Eddie. "I guess that's it."

"Yes, Eddie, that's it," said his father. "Good-by!"

"By!" said Eddie, as he hung up the telephone.

"Such a swell dog!" said Joe. "It's a shame to send him to the shelter."

"Maybe if we gave him a bath and combed him, he would look so nice Dad would change his mind," said Eddie.

"You can try," said Rudy, "but I don't think it will work."

"Let's hurry," said Eddie. "Let's get him washed."

"He's so big," said Frank. "Where can we wash him?"

"He's too big for the washtub in the basement," said Rudy.

"Guess we'll have to wash him in the bathtub," said Joe.

"Well, let's hurry," said Eddie.

But the dog had disappeared! "Now where is he?" said Eddie. Eddie's brothers looked around. There was no dog in sight.

"Call him," said Frank.

"How can I call him?" said Eddie. "I don't know his name."

"Here, dog! Here, dog!" Rudy called.

"Here, Rex! Here, Rex!" Joe called.

51

"Here, Fido! Here, Fido!" Frank called.

No dog appeared.

Eddie went into the sun porch. He began looking behind and under the furniture. He soon found the dog crouched behind a big chair. "Come on, boy," said Eddie. "Here he is," he called to his brothers. "Come help me. I can't drag him out 'cause he hasn't any handle. No collar to get hold of."

"I'll get him," said Rudy.

Rudy came. He tried to move the dog. It was like trying to move a broken-down truck. The dog wouldn't budge.

"We have to hurry," said Eddie. "Dad will be home before we can get him washed."

"You can't hurry this dog," said Rudy. "You can't even move him."

"We'll have to carry him upstairs," said Frank. "Come on. Everybody help!"

"I better go up and run the water in the bathtub," said Eddie. "Then you can put him right in."

As Eddie started up the stairs, he said, "You know what I would call that dog if he were mine? I'd call him Reds! I'd say, 'Here, Reds! Here, Reds!' "

The dog suddenly leaped to his feet, almost knocking Eddie's three brothers over. He flew after Eddie like a rocket. As Eddie dashed up the stairs, the dog followed.

"His name must be Reds!" Eddie called down to his brothers.

Eddie turned on the water in the bathtub, but when the dog heard the water, he sneaked away again. He went into Eddie's room and hid under the bed. The boys soon found him, but the dog was deaf to coaxing. He kept his chin on the floor and growled.

"He'll never come out from under the bed, Eddie," said Joe.

"If he won't come out from under the bed," said

Eddie, coming into his room, "We'll have to move the bed. Then he won't be under it any more."

"O.K.!" said the twins.

"It won't work," said Rudy, as he took hold of one side of the headboard. They pushed and pulled but they did not uncover the dog. He crawled along on his belly and kept out of sight.

"I'll never get him washed before Dad comes in," said Eddie.

Just then Eddie heard the front door open. He was sure it was his father.

The dog, under the bed, heard a footstep in the hall below. He pricked up his ears. Then he flew out from under the bed, dashed down the stairs, and with squeals and woofs, jumped all over Eddie's father as he tried to hang his coat in the hall closet.

The four boys upstairs hung over the banisters and watched the performance. Eddie's heart was in his mouth.

"Down! Down!" he heard his father say. "What a dirty mutt!"

"He isn't a mutt, Dad," Eddie called down. "He's a golden retriever. I'm sure he is."

"Well, the people who own him can retrieve him from the shelter," said his father. "He isn't going to spend one night in this house. Not one night."

Mr. Wilson went into the living room and sat down in his chair. He looked over his mail. Meanwhile, the dog ran all around him, sniffing at his shoes and wagging his tail.

Eddie and his brothers came downstairs and into the living room. "He likes you, Dad," said Eddie.

"Humph!" said his father.

Suddenly the dog ran out of the room and up the stairs. Eddie could hear him running around each of the bedrooms.

Mr. Wilson looked up. "Now listen to him. Tearing the house apart."

Just as Eddie got up to see what the dog was doing, he heard him coming down the stairs.

In a moment, to everyone's great surprise, the dog trotted into the living room, carrying one of Mr. Wilson's house slippers. He brought it right to Mr. Wilson and laid it at his feet. Then he went upstairs again. In a flash he was back with the other slipper.

Mr. Wilson looked at the dog in surprise. Then a wide smile spread across his face. "Well!" he said. "Isn't he a nice dog!" Mr. Wilson reached out and patted the dog on the head.

Eddie looked at his brothers, and his brothers looked at Eddie. They all grinned. Just then Mrs. Wilson called them all to dinner. When they were seated at the table, Eddie said, "Have you something to feed the dog, Mother?"

"Oh, they will feed the dog at the shelter," said Mrs. Wilson.

"At the shelter!" exclaimed Mr. Wilson. "Do you think I would let a nice dog like that go to the shelter?"

The boys looked at their father. In a chorus they said, "No!" Then they began to eat their dinner.

As Eddie lifted a piece of meat on his fork, he was surprised to see a large drop of water fall on his plate. Then another drop splashed beside his mashed potatoes. Eddie looked up at the ceiling. There was water on the ceiling.

Suddenly Eddie remembered the bathtub. He jumped up from his chair. " 'Scuse me!" he said. He rushed out of the dining room and up the stairs. When he reached the second floor, water was running out of the bathroom into the hall. The bathroom floor was a small pond, and a waterfall was pouring over the side of the tub.

Eddie splashed through the water and turned off the faucets.

By this time his mother had discovered the water dropping from the dining-room ceiling. She came upstairs, followed by Mr. Wilson. "Whatever is the matter?" she called to Eddie.

"It's O.K.!" Eddie shouted from the bathroom. "I guess I forgot to turn off the water when I thought we were going to wash the dog."

"You guess you did?" said his mother. "You mean you did forget. Now look at this mess!"

"I'm sorry, Mother," said Eddie. "I'm awfully sorry."

"I want that dog taken to the shelter tonight," said his mother. "He has caused enough trouble."

Eddie's father cleared his throat. "Why, it isn't the dog's fault that the water in the tub overflowed," he said.

Eddie's mother turned to his father and said, "You were the one who said, 'No more dogs'!" Then she looked right up into his face and said, very slowly, "I believe you want to keep it."

"I never had a dog that fetched my slippers before," said Mr. Wilson.

Now Eddie knew that the dog would stay. He would stay until they found the owner and there was a chance, of course, that it might be "Finders Keepers."

Everyone set to work mopping up the water.

"Boys are the limit," said Mrs. Wilson. "And so are fathers!"

CHAPTER 4

EDDIE GOES FOR HIS PARROT

ON SATURDAY morning, as soon as breakfast was over, Eddie said to his mother, "When can we go to the hotel to get Louella?"

"Oh, I forgot about Louella," said his mother. "I don't believe we can get her today, because your father has gone off with the car."

"I don't think I should leave Louella at the hotel all day today," said Eddie.

"You could go into town on the bus," said his mother, "and bring her home on the bus."

"I guess that would be better than leaving her there until tomorrow," said Eddie.

"The Number Four bus that you get at the corner stops right in front of the hotel," said Mrs. Wilson.

"Sure! I know," replied Eddie.

Mrs. Wilson gave Eddie his bus fare and he started off. When he reached the hotel, the doorman recognized him. "Hello, young man," he said. "I suppose you have come for your parrot."

"That's right!" said Eddie.

"I hope you won't have as much trouble getting out of the door as you had coming in," said the doorman with a chuckle.

"That was something, wasn't it?" said Eddie.

65

"What happened to that dog?" said the doorman.

"We took him home," said Eddie. "We looked in the Lost and Found ads in the paper, but we didn't see any ad for a golden retriever."

"So that's what it is," said the doorman. "Well, I hope you find the owner. Probably get a reward."

"I don't think they deserve to get him back," said Eddie. "People who don't put a collar on a nice dog like that don't deserve to get him back. I'm going to buy him a collar."

"You go up to the fifth floor for your parrot," said the doorman.

"Thanks!" said Eddie.

Eddie took the elevator to the fifth floor. "Where do I get my parrot?" he said to the elevator boy, when he opened the door.

"Right over in that cloakroom," the elevator boy replied, pointing to an open door.

When Eddie went into the room, he saw two parrots in their cages, sitting side by side. There was no one in charge of the room, so Eddie picked up the cage that had his tag tied to it. "Come along, Louella," said Eddie. "How did you like the ball?"

"Yawk!" said the parrot.

"You can talk better than that," said Eddie, as he carried the cage to the elevator.

Eddie pushed the button for the elevator and waited. While he waited he could hear the one remaining parrot rattling its cage and beating its wings. It was raising a terrible fuss.

"I guess that other parrot is lonely," said Eddie, as he stepped into the elevator.

"You're sure you picked up the right bird?" the elevator boy asked.

Eddie laughed. "Oh, sure! My name is right here on this tag."

"O.K.!" said the boy.

When Eddie reached the front door the doorman said, "You sure you've got the right bird?"

"Sure!" said Eddie. "See—here is my name on the tag."

"Good!" said the doorman, as Eddie stepped into the revolving door. "Now, easy does it!" said the doorman, as he gave the door a push. "Don't get hooked."

Eddie got out without getting hooked. He set the cage down on the pavement and took the cover for the cage out of his pocket. He put the cover over the cage. "Yawk!" said the parrot.

"This is just for while we're on the bus," said Eddie.

The parrot chattered under the cover, while Eddie waited for the bus.

Soon the bus came, and Eddie stepped in. When he handed his fare to the driver, the driver said, "What have you got there? Animals can't ride on the buses."

"It isn't an animal," said Eddie. "It's a bird."

"It's alive, isn't it?" said the bus driver.

"Sure, it's alive," said Eddie. "It's my parrot, Lou-ella."

"Anything alive that isn't a person is an animal, according to bus regulations," said the driver. "Here's your fare back. Get off."

"But I have to get home," said Eddie.

"I can't help that," said the driver. "I have to obey my orders—no animals on the bus."

Eddie stepped off the bus. As he did so, the parrot said, in a high, sharp voice, "Hiya, chum! Do you like your coffee?"

Eddie was so surprised he nearly dropped the cage.

"Who said that?" said the bus driver.

"She did!" said Eddie, pointing to the cage.

"Well, now! That's different," said the bus driver. "Anything that can talk isn't an animal. Get on."

Eddie got on. He paid his fare and sat down.

Again there came from under the cover of the cage, "Hiya, chum! Do you like your coffee?"

Eddie was surprised that Louella could have learned so much overnight at a ball.

Everyone on the bus laughed when they heard the parrot talk.

The man sitting beside Eddie said, "What is your parrot's name?"

"Louella," Eddie replied. "I brought her home with me from Texas. Then she only said one thing."

"What was that?" the man asked.

"She just said, 'Texas is better,' " Eddie answered.

The man laughed.

"Pickle-push! Pickle-push!" came from inside the cage.

Eddie looked surprised. "She sure learned a lot of new words overnight," he said. "She's been at the ball at

72

the hotel. Just for decoration. Those parrots must have talked all night."

"What else does she say?" the man asked.

"Oh, she calls my mother Pretty Girl," said Eddie.

"I'll bet your mother likes that," said the man.

"Hit her again!" cried the parrot.

This made Eddie lift the cover and look at the bird. "What's the matter with you?" he said. There was no reply.

Eddie dropped the cover and went on talking to the man beside him. "She says, 'Eddie is best!' " said Eddie. "That's me."

"I guess she is real fond of you," said the man.

"Nuts!" said the parrot.

"I was a little bit afraid to lend her for a decoration," said Eddie, " 'cause I wouldn't want to lose her."

"I should think not!" said the man.

"Rats!" came from inside the cage.

"Louella doesn't like cats," said Eddie.

75

"Oh! I thought she said *rats,*" said the man.

"No, it just sounded like *rats,*" said Eddie, as he turned to look out of the window. "Next stop is mine," he said. He reached up and pulled the cord. "Well, so long!" he said to the man beside him.

"Good-by!" said the man. "Take good care of Louella."

"You bet!" replied Eddie.

When Eddie got home he carried the cage into the sun porch and hung it on the stand by the window. He took the cover off and said, "Hello, Louella! Who's best?"

"Yawk!" was the reply.

"Who's best, Louella?" said Eddie.

"Nuts!" said the bird.

Then the twins came into the room. "So the dumb bird is back from the ball!" said Frank. "Hi, Louella!"

"Pickle-push!" said the parrot.

"Oh! She has learned a new word!" said Frank.

"It's about time!" said Joe.

"Hiya, chum!" said the bird.

"Did you hear that?" said Joe. "She's getting real smart."

Eddie was beginning to look a little bit worried. It didn't seem possible that Louella could have picked up so many new words overnight.

Eddie called to his mother. "Mother," he said, "there is something awful funny about Louella."

Mrs. Wilson came into the room. "What is the matter with her?" she said.

"She is saying things she never said before, and she won't say anything she used to say," Eddie explained.

Mrs. Wilson came over to the cage. "Here's Pretty Girl, Louella," said Eddie. "See Pretty Girl?"

"Yawk!" said the parrot. "Old Sourpuss!"

At this point, Eddie let out a yell like an Indian.

"This isn't Louella. It isn't Louella. They gave me some other parrot. I know it isn't Louella."

Just then Sidney Stewart, who lived next door, came in. "What's the matter?" she said.

"Sid!" exclaimed Eddie. "They mixed up the parrots down at the hotel last night. This isn't Louella."

Sidney looked at the parrot. "It looks like Louella," she said.

"But it doesn't talk like Louella," said Eddie. "It just called my mother Old Sourpuss! Do you think Louella would call my mother Old Sourpuss?"

"You better take this bird back right away," said Frank, who was beginning to feel sorry about Louella. He was really quite fond of Eddie's parrot. He didn't want anything to happen to her.

"I have to go all the way back in the bus again," said Eddie, "and the bus driver didn't want to let me on with the parrot."

"Maybe my mother would drive us down to the hotel," said Sidney. "I'll ask her."

Sidney ran home and in a few minutes she was back. "Come on, Eddie!" she said. "My mother says she will drive us down."

Eddie lifted the cage off the hook and carried it out to the car. "Look, Mrs. Stewart!" he said. "It's the right cage but the wrong parrot."

Eddie and Sidney climbed into the front seat beside Mrs. Stewart. Eddie held the cage on his lap. "I hope Louella is still there," he said.

"I am sure you will find her," said Mrs. Stewart.

Eddie could hardly wait to get back to the hotel. Every time they stopped for a red light, he would say under his breath, "Turn green! Turn green!"

At last Mrs. Stewart drove up in front of the hotel and stopped. Eddie jumped out and ran to the front door with the cage in his hand. Sidney followed him.

He went through the revolving door like a pin wheel, and there was the doorman again.

"What's brought you and your parrot back?" he said.

"It's not my parrot," said Eddie. "This is the wrong parrot."

"It has the name *Edward Wilson* on the tag," said the man, reading the tag.

"Oh, it's the right cage," said Eddie, "but this isn't Louella."

"How do you know?" the doorman asked.

"I know because this parrot doesn't say anything that Louella says," Eddie replied. "It talks, but it doesn't talk like Louella."

"Take it up to the fifth floor," said the doorman.

Eddie and Sidney got into the elevator. When the elevator boy saw Eddie and the parrot, he said, "So you're back again!"

"This is the wrong parrot," Eddie replied.

80

"Oh, that's too bad," said the boy.

Eddie and Sidney stepped off at the fifth floor, and Eddie led the way to the cloakroom and looked around. The long table where the parrots' cages had stood was bare. The racks and the shelves were empty.

Eddie stood holding the parrot's cage, looking dejected. "Oh!" he said. "They are all gone."

"Oh, dear!" said Sidney. "What will you do now?"

"I don't know," said Eddie, as he turned to go back to the elevator. "I guess I better take care of this one, because whoever has Louella has lost this bird."

"Just as soon as Louella begins to talk, they will know they have the wrong parrot," said Sidney. "Then they will bring her back."

"I hope so," said Eddie. "Poor Louella! No wonder she was making such a fuss when I walked out with this parrot."

Downstairs, Eddie explained everything to the doorman. He was very sympathetic. "I don't know how it could have happened," he said. "But don't worry. Whoever has Louella will bring her back. Then I'll tell them that you have their parrot. Everything will be straightened out."

Eddie returned home feeling hopeful but not very happy.

CHAPTER 5

EDDIE TELLS THE NEWS

Eddie waited impatiently to hear that Louella had been returned to the hotel, but by bedtime on Saturday night he had heard nothing. "Don't you think it's funny I haven't heard anything about Louella?" he said to his mother.

"You will probably hear tomorrow," said his mother.

"Many people are out all day on Saturday. Perhaps they haven't noticed that they have the wrong parrot."

"I hope they notice soon," said Eddie.

"Just go to sleep," said his mother. "Louella will come back."

Eddie waited all day Sunday, but there was no word. In the afternoon he telephoned to the hotel and asked to speak to the doorman.

When the doorman said hello, Eddie said, "This is Eddie Wilson. Do you remember me?"

"Sure!" said the doorman. "You're the fellow that got the wrong parrot."

"That's right," said Eddie. "Have you heard anything?"

"Not a word," said the doorman. "Seems funny, but perhaps she hasn't said anything."

"I wish she would begin to talk," said Eddie. "She talks plenty at home."

"I guess maybe she feels shy," said the doorman.

"Maybe!" said Eddie. "You'll call me as soon as you hear, won't you?"

"Sure will!" said the doorman.

"Thanks!" said Eddie, and he hung up.

When Eddie went to school on Monday he had big news. He now had a lost dog and the wrong parrot. Eddie went around among his friends saying, "Wait until I tell you about my parrot, Louella!" If they didn't show any interest, he would say, "Wait until I tell you about the swell dog I found. He's a golden retriever, I think."

"I knew somebody who lost a golden retriever once," said his friend Anna Patricia. "I'll bet it's theirs."

Eddie was immediately sorry he had mentioned the dog. "Oh, I don't think it is," he said.

"I'll bet it is," said Anna Patricia. "I'll bet you have their dog."

"What color was their dog?" Eddie asked.

"Why, golden, of course!" said Anna Patricia. "It was a golden retriever, like you said."

"Well, this dog is red," said Eddie.

"Now I remember—their dog was sort of red," said Anna Patricia.

"How big was it?" Eddie asked.

"Oh, not very big. About as big as a cocker spaniel," said Anna Patricia.

"Ho! This dog is much bigger than a cocker spaniel," said Eddie.

"Of course it is, now," said Anna Patricia. "It has grown."

"Where do these people live?" Eddie asked.

"They live in Australia," said Anna Patricia.

"In Australia!" Eddie exclaimed. "How do you think I could find their dog if they live in Australia? Do you think he dropped down out of a sputnik?"

"Oh, they didn't live in Australia when they lost their dog," said Anna Patricia.

"You think you know so much, Annie Pat," said Eddie. "Maybe you know who the parrot belongs to that I have instead of Louella."

"What is the parrot's name that you have?" Anna Patricia asked.

"How do I know!" replied Eddie. "It hasn't told me."

"Well, I wouldn't know unless I knew its name," said Anna Patricia.

"You didn't know the dog's name," said Eddie, "but you are sure he belongs to somebody in Australia."

"You are just trying to mix me up," said Anna Patricia.

"Mix you up!" exclaimed Eddie. "Annie Pat, you are so mixed up, you are like scrambled eggs."

"Just for that, Eddie Wilson, I am not going to help you find your parrot," said Anna Patricia. "And I had a very good idea."

87

Anna Patricia walked off, swinging her curls.

Eddie's friend Boodles Cary had come along and had heard what Eddie said about his parrot. "I'll help you find Louella," said Boodles. "I'm going to be a detective when I grow up. I'm studying it now. I have a book that tells all about it. I'll help you, Eddie."

Boodles pulled a little notebook out of his hip pocket. He pulled a pencil out of the pocket of his jacket. "This is my book for writing down clues," he said. "Now shoot! Give me a description of this bird. What color hair? I mean what color feathers?"

"Green," said Eddie.

"Eyes?" said Boodles.

"Yellow," said Eddie.

"Yellow?" said Boodles. "Are you sure? I never heard of yellow eyes except in cats."

"They were yellow," said Eddie.

Boodles wrote everything down in his notebook.

88

"How tall?" was his next question. "About as big as my ruler," said Eddie.

"How much does she weigh?" said Boodles.

"I never weighed her," Eddie replied.

"O.K.! Skip it!" said Boodles. "When was she last seen?"

"The last time I saw her I didn't know it was Louella," said Eddie.

"You didn't know it was Louella!" exclaimed Boodles.

"If I had known, I would have picked her up instead of the one I have now," said Eddie.

"Oh!" said Boodles. "This is a hard case. If you didn't know her she must have been wearing a disguise."

"Are you crazy!" exclaimed Eddie.

"The trouble with you, Eddie," said Boodles, "is that you don't know anything about detective work. My book tells all about disguises. You would be surprised how kidnapers disguise people."

"I don't think Louella was kidnaped," said Eddie.

"All the same, she was birdnaped," said Boodles.

"I think it was some kind of a mistake," said Eddie. "Somehow, the birds got into the wrong cages."

"Hah!" said Boodles. "Then somebody must have let them out of their cages. There's a clue to work on."

"It won't help to find Louella, just finding out who let the birds out of their cages," said Eddie.

"Oh, Eddie!" said Boodles. "I can see you don't know anything about detective work. You will never find your parrot." Boodles walked off.

At recess, Eddie told his friend Dumpty Peterson about the mixed-up parrots. "Did you tell Mr. Kilpatrick?" was the first thing Dumpty asked.

Mr. Kilpatrick was the policeman who directed the traffic on the wide street near the school. He was a

friend to all the children. They believed that Mr. Kilpatrick could solve any problem.

"No, I didn't," said Eddie. "I guess that is a good idea."

"Sure it is," said Dumpty. "I think somebody should get arrested."

"Who?" said Eddie.

"I don't know," said Dumpty, "but somebody should. Somebody down at that hotel."

As soon as school was out, Eddie dashed off to tell his story to Mr. Kilpatrick. He found Mr. Kilpatrick busy with the traffic and with the little children. Mr. Kilpatrick always took the children across the street.

"Don't bother me now, Eddie," said Mr. Kilpatrick. "If you want to tell me something, go sit in my car until I am through with this job."

While he was waiting for Mr. Kilpatrick, Eddie decided that he would tell Mr. Kilpatrick all about the mixed-up parrots, but he would not tell him about the dog. Eddie wanted to keep the dog. He didn't want to find the owner. Maybe they would give a reward, but Eddie felt he would rather have the dog. This was the nicest dog he had ever found and, best of all, his father liked this dog.

Finally Mr. Kilpatrick was finished with the traffic. The last child from school had been taken across the big wide street. Mr. Kilpatrick walked over to his red car and said, "Well, Eddie! What is your trouble to-day?"

"I've got parrot trouble," said Eddie.

"Parrot trouble!" exclaimed Mr. Kilpatrick. "Let's hear the story."

Eddie recounted the whole story of the two parrots. When he had finished he told Mr. Kilpatrick how Dumpty had said, "Somebody ought to be arrested. Somebody down at that hotel."

"I wouldn't know who to arrest," said Mr. Kilpatrick. "If somebody stole your parrot, I could arrest him. Or if somebody was hiding your parrot so that you couldn't get her, I could arrest him."

"Oh!" said Eddie. "You mean, well, just for instance, if I found a nice dog and I kept him so that the owners couldn't find him, that I would get arrested?"

"Well, you wouldn't exactly go to jail for it, but the owner could bring you into court if he found out you had his dog."

"I just said for instance," said Eddie.

"Oh, sure! Sure!" said Mr. Kilpatrick. "I know if you found a dog, you would try to find the owner."

Eddie thought about this for a minute. Then he opened the door of Mr. Kilpatrick's car and jumped out. "Well, thanks, Mr. Kilpatrick!" he said. "If you hear anything about my parrot, will you let me know?"

"I certainly will," Mr. Kilpatrick replied. "And if you find any dogs, let me know."

"What if it doesn't have any collar on?" Eddie asked.

"I still think you should try to find the owners," said Mr. Kilpatrick. "Maybe they would be missing their dog just as much as you are missing Louella."

"Maybe!" said Eddie. "I hadn't thought of that."

CHAPTER 6

LOUELLA TAKES A RIDE

MEANWHILE, Louella had been carried off to the other side of town to a boy named Tommy Tomkins. Tommy had had his parrot longer than Eddie had owned Louella. Tommy couldn't remember a time when he didn't have his parrot. The parrot's name was

Pauline, but she had been called Sourpuss so long that everyone had forgotten her name was Pauline.

Tommy's grandfather had been a sea captain and he had brought Pauline from Africa. He had taught her to talk. She talked like a rowdy, but she was really a nice bird and Tommy was very fond of her.

The Tomkinses were getting ready to move when Pauline went to the ball at the hotel. Tommy's mother thought it a great nuisance to take Pauline over to the hotel at such a time, but Tommy's father knew the manager and had promised to lend the parrot.

It was Mr. Tomkins who went to the hotel to pick up Pauline on Saturday afternoon. He got there just twenty minutes after Eddie had left with his bird cage. Mr. Tomkins picked up the only parrot that was left. He looked at the tag fastened to the top of the cage and saw that it said *Tomkins*. On his way out, Mr. Tomkins said, "Well, that's the last of the parrots."

"No more up there?" said the doorman.

"This was the only one," replied Mr. Tomkins, as he went through the revolving door. When he reached home, he carried the parrot into the room which used to be called Tommy's playroom, but which Tommy now called his den.

Just as Mr. Tomkins was hanging the cage on the stand by the window, Tommy came into the room. "Oh!" he cried. "Here's good old Sourpuss! Did you have a good time at the ball, Sourpuss?"

There was no reply.

Tommy tried all the tricks that had always made Pauline talk, but she might as well have been deaf.

At dinner that evening, Tommy said, "I don't know what is the matter with old Sourpuss. She won't say a word."

"Cat's got her tongue!" his father said with a laugh.

Sunday was a busy day for the Tomkinses, for the

moving van was coming early on Monday morning. The company Mr. Tomkins worked for was moving him to a new office, three hundred miles away. No one paid any attention to the parrot. In fact, they were all glad that she kept quiet.

On Monday morning the moving van arrived at eight o'clock. It took the moving men all day to pack the big van. When Tommy's father came home at five o'clock, there was nothing left in the house but some cartons, the suitcases, and the parrot. These were to go with Mr. and Mrs. Tomkins and Tommy in the car.

By six o'clock the car was packed and they were ready to leave. The parrot's cage sat on top of the cartons that were piled on the back seat of the car. She had not said anything but "Yawk!" for three days.

When Tommy was settled between his father and mother, on the front seat of the car, he said, "I don't know what is the matter with old Sourpuss! She hasn't said a word since Dad brought her home. Do you think she ate something at the ball that upset her?"

"No," replied his father. "Maybe she is upset over the moving."

"I don't know why!" said Mrs. Tomkins. "I didn't see her packing any cartons or suitcases. She just sat and said, 'Yawk!' "

"Maybe she just tired herself out watching everyone else work," said Mr. Tomkins.

"Poor Sourpuss!" said Tommy.

"Where shall we spend the night?" asked Tommy's mother.

"There is a nice motel about an hour's drive from here," said Mr. Tomkins. "We can have dinner and spend the night there. Then we can get an early start tomorrow morning."

"We won't leave Sourpuss in the car, will we?" Tommy asked.

"Oh, no!" replied his father. "We'll take her inside."

A little after seven o'clock, the Tomkinses drove up to the motel. Mr. Tomkins parked the car in front of one of the little white cabins. He went into the office and came back with the key to the cabin. Tommy and his mother got out of the car. Mr. Tomkins carried the bags into the cabin and Tommy carried the parrot's cage.

Tommy gave the parrot some food before he left with his father and mother for dinner. After a good dinner the Tomkinses returned to their little cabin and went to bed. They were all very tired.

Mr. Tomkins' alarm clock went off very early the following morning. It woke up all the Tomkinses. Tommy thought it was the middle of the night, for it was still dark. He rolled over and was almost asleep again when his mother shook his shoulder and said, "Come, Tommy! It's time to get up. We have a long drive today." Tommy rubbed his eyes and crawled out of bed.

Before long Mr. Tomkins was carrying the bags out to the car.

Tommy stepped out of the door with the parrot's cage in his hand. The early-morning air was sharp. Tommy looked up at the sky and was surprised to see the stars. He didn't remember ever having seen the stars in the morning before. He had never been up and out so early. It was so quiet that it made Tommy feel as if he and his father and mother were the only people awake in the whole world.

Mr. Tomkins put the bags in the trunk of the car. Then he said, "Tommy, put the parrot down. I think we can repack the cartons on the back seat so that they will be more steady."

"O.K.!" said Tommy.

Tommy looked around for a place to set down the cage. There was a small truck parked beside the Tomkinses' car. The rear end was right beside Tommy. Tommy put the cage on the floor of the truck.

It took Tommy and his father about ten minutes to repack the cartons and boxes. Just as they finished, Mrs. Tomkins came out of the cabin. "Come along, boys," she whispered. "It will soon be daylight."

"Where do we get our breakfast?" Tommy whispered.

"We'll stop somewhere along the way," said his father, "at about half past seven."

"Come along, Tommy! Hop in," said his mother.

Tommy hopped in and slid over to the center of the front seat. His mother got in beside him. Mr. Tomkins got behind the wheel and they started off.

"I guess we are the only people on the road," said Tommy.

"No," replied his father, "there is a headlight coming up over the hill, just ahead."

"It's a truck," said Tommy. "I can tell by the way it roars."

As the truck passed, the driver waved his hand to the Tomkinses. They waved back. "I guess everybody feels friendly so early in the morning," remarked Tommy.

Meanwhile, Louella was sitting in the back of the little truck outside of the motel. It was dark, so she went to sleep.

About ten minutes later, the owner of the truck came out of one of the nearby cabins. He was a young man and he softly whistled a gay tune. He threw a little black bag upon the front seat and climbed in. He started the motor and stepped on the gas pedal. The truck seemed to leap forward. This bounced Louella's cage, and Louella woke up.

"Yawk!" cried Louella. "Yawk!"

The man in the truck didn't hear. He pressed his

foot down on the accelerator and the truck fairly flew along the road. Louella bounced higher and higher. The water splashed out of her water cup and her seed flew all around. Poor Louella could not sit on her perch and she could not sit on the bottom of the cage. She clung to the bars of the cage and trembled. Her whole world shook and bounced as though an earthquake had struck it.

The little truck sped along, passing the few cars that were on the road.

Before long Mr. Tomkins said, "I can see a car coming, and it is certainly traveling fast."

In a few minutes he said, "It's a little truck, I think."

In a moment, the little truck was beside the Tomkinses' car and was passing it. "He certainly is going somewhere mighty fast," said Mr. Tomkins.

"This is the time of day to travel," Mrs. Tomkins said.

The little truck was so far ahead now that it looked as small as a firefly. Soon it was out of sight of the Tomkinses.

Louella was too frightened now to say even a weak "Yawk!"

Suddenly the truck hit a deep hole in the road. Louella's cage bounced higher than ever. It bounced right out of the back of the truck. When it hit the road, it rolled over and over and finally came to rest on the shoulder of the road. Poor Louella! It was something like going over Niagara Falls in a barrel.

Now that solid ground was under her and everything had stopped shaking, Louella let go of the bars of her cage. A squirrel ran past her.

"Cats!" said Louella.

In a very short time, the headlights of the Tomkinses' car shone on the parrot's cage. The glitter of gilt caught Tommy's eye, but only for a moment.

The car passed by, leaving Louella in the darkness again.

"Dad!" said Tommy. "Did you see something gold beside the road, back there?"

"Something caught my eye for a moment," his father replied.

"Maybe we should have stopped," said Tommy. "Maybe it was something valuable."

"Shall we go back and take a look?" said his father.

"Oh, don't let's go back!" his mother exclaimed. "It will soon be daylight and then the heavy traffic will start."

"But it may be something valuable," said Tommy.

"It will only take fifteen minutes," said Mr. Tomkins.

"All right," said his mother, "if you want to go back."

Mr. Tomkins turned the car around and started

back. "Now, Tommy," he said, "you will have to keep a sharp lookout, because whatever it is, it is not on our side of the road now."

"I'm watching," said Tommy. "It isn't as dark as it was. I think I'll see it."

Going back seemed to take much longer. Finally Mr. Tomkins said, "I am afraid we have passed it. I don't think it was this far back."

"I think we are just wasting time," said Mrs. Tomkins.

But just then Tommy cried out, "There it is!"

Mr. Tomkins stepped on his brake and brought the car to a stop. He opened the car door and stepped out. Tommy slid under the wheel and got out beside his father.

"Run across and take a look," said his father.

Tommy ran across the road. When he looked he couldn't believe his eyes.

"What is it?" his father called to him.

"Why! Why! It looks like Sourpuss!" Tommy called back.

Mr. Tomkins turned to his wife and said, "Isn't the parrot on the back seat of the car?"

Mrs. Tomkins turned around and looked on the back seat. "Indeed she is not!" she replied.

Mr. Tomkins ran across the road to Tommy. "She's not on the back seat," he said, "but how did she get here?"

"I remember now," said Tommy. "When you asked me to help you repack the cartons, I set the cage in the back of a little truck that was standing beside our car. I guess I forgot to put her in the car."

"I guess you did," said Mr. Tomkins. "But are you sure this is Sourpuss?"

Tommy picked up the cage and held it up for his father to see. "Well, it looks like Sourpuss and the cage

118

looks like our cage, only it's sorta out of shape," said Tommy.

"Perhaps that little truck that passed us was the truck you put her in," said his father. "At the speed he was going, if he hit a hole in the road, it could have bounced the cage right out."

"I'll bet that was what happened," said Tommy, as he and his father started back to the car.

When they reached the car, Tommy said to his mother, "Now isn't it a good thing we came back? Poor old Sourpuss! We would have lost her forever."

"Of course I am glad we came back," said Mrs. Tomkins. "I wouldn't want to lose the old girl."

Tommy placed the cage on top of the cartons in the back of the car. Then he slid back under the wheel beside his mother.

Soon the car was turned around and they were off again. Dawn had come now and suddenly all of the electric lights along the road went out. Tommy turned and looked back at the parrot. "I'm glad we didn't lose old Sourpuss," he said.

"Yawk!" said Louella. "Eddie is best!"

Mrs. Tomkins turned and looked at the parrot. "What did she say?" Mrs. Tomkins asked.

"I never heard her say that before," said Tommy. "It sounded like 'Eddie is best!' "

"My goodness!" exclaimed Tommy's mother. "Maybe it isn't Sourpuss after all!"

"Of course it is Sourpuss!" said Mr. Tomkins. "What other parrot would be out here at this time of the morning?"

CHAPTER 7

THE SPECIAL-DELIVERY LETTER

BY THE end of the week, the Tomkinses were settled in their house and Tommy was in the fourth grade in his new school. Tommy had watched his parrot carefully all during the week, and he was certain now that it was not Sourpuss. This parrot looked like Sourpuss, but she did not act like Sourpuss or talk like Sourpuss.

121

Tommy could see that this parrot was much more lady-like. Once Tommy thought she said, "Hello, Pretty Girl!" Sourpuss would never have said that.

The story of the parrot's wild ride and of how she was picked up on the road was a wonderful tale for Tommy to tell to his new classmates. Everyone was impressed, especially when Tommy said he was sure this parrot was not Sourpuss. He told the whole story about the ball at the hotel, and how people loaned their parrots for the decorations, to everyone who would listen. He told it to the mailman, the milkman, the grocery man, the man who drove the school bus, and the school janitor.

All the children in Tommy's class were interested in what they called "The Sourpuss Mystery." There were two theories. Some of the children thought there had been a mix-up at the hotel. Others believed that the parrot Tommy now had was not the parrot Tommy had set down in the back of the truck early in the morning, outside of the motel.

The whole story about Sourpuss was published in the school paper and the entire school talked about Tommy's parrot. Tommy felt very important when the big boys came up to him at recess and said, "Hi, Tommy! Hear anything about your parrot?"

By the end of the week Mr. and Mrs. Tomkins, as well as Tommy, were certain that the parrot they had picked up on the road was not old Sourpuss. Mr. Tomkins said he would write a letter to the manager of the hotel and tell him that they had the wrong parrot.

"Whoever has Sourpuss, must know that she is not their parrot," said Mr. Tomkins.

"I bet they have told the hotel about it," said Tommy.

"No doubt!" said his father. "They will be just as happy to get this bird as we will be to get old Sourpuss back."

"This parrot keeps saying, 'What's cookin',' " said Tommy.

"And I guess Sourpuss is asking the people she is with if they like their coffee," said Mr. Tomkins.

"Poor old Sourpuss!" said Tommy. "I guess they don't give her any coffee, and she likes her coffee so much."

"How about your writing the letter, Tommy?" said his father. "After all, Sourpuss is your parrot."

"All right," said Tommy. "I'll write it."

Tommy sat down at his desk. He pulled out a sheet of paper. Then he picked up his pen and said, "Who do I write to?"

"You write to Mr. John Morgan," said his father, "the Parkview Hotel."

Tommy got a big blot of ink on his first letter, so he had to write another one. When he finally finished it, he handed it to his father, who read it aloud.

Dear Mr. Morgan,

I have the wrong parrot. we got the wrong one after the Ball, we think. Did anybody ask about getting a wrong parrot? Because somebody has my parrot called Sourpuss. We have moved and you will see our new address on the envelope. Please answer soon.

Very truly yours,
Tommy Tomkins

P.S. Her name really isn't Sourpuss. it is Pauline, but we have always called her Sourpuss, and I don't think she knows her name is Pauline.

"How is it?" said Tommy, after his father had read the letter.

"It is a very good letter," said his father. "Now address the envelope and we can get it off. We had better send it by special delivery."

Tommy addressed the envelope to Mr. Morgan at the Hotel Parkview. He sealed it and stuck a stamp on the corner. Then he put the special-delivery stamp beside the other one. He ran to the mailbox at the corner and dropped the letter through the slot.

The next day Eddie stopped at the hotel to inquire about news of Louella. When the doorman saw Eddie, he said, "No news yet, son, but I am sure we shall hear something soon."

"I don't know why the people who have Louella haven't telephoned," said Eddie. "They must know now that they have the wrong parrot."

126

Dear Mr. Morgan,

I have the wrong Parrot.
we got the wrong one after the Ball,
we think. Did anybody ask about getting
a wrong Parrot?
Because somebody has my parrot
called Sourpuss. We have moved
and you will see our new address
on the envelope.
Please answer soon.

Very truly yours,
Tommy Tomkins

P.S. Her name really isn't Sourpuss.
it is Pauline, but we have always
called her Sourpuss, and I don't
think she knows her name is
Pauline.

"I'm sure we'll get some word soon," said the doorman.

"I sure hope so!" said Eddie. "So long."

When Eddie left, the doorman walked over to the bell captain's desk and whispered to him, "Something went wrong with those parrots at the ball."

"The parrots?" said the bell captain. "What do you mean, 'something went wrong with them'?"

"Looks like a couple of them got mixed up," said the doorman.

"No!" exclaimed the bell captain. "That isn't possible. Those birds weren't out of their cages."

The doorman shrugged his shoulders and said, "All I know is a fellow named Eddie Wilson claims he has the wrong parrot."

"Ridiculous!" said the bell captain. "Whatever gave him that idea?"

"The parrot gave him that idea," said the doorman.

"The parrot can talk and the parrot's talk is all wrong. It doesn't say anything it said before the ball and it says a lot Eddie never heard out of the mouth of his parrot. There was a mix-up, if you ask me!"

The bell captain let out a low whistle. "Mighty funny we haven't heard from the people who got this fellow's parrot," he said.

"I have been hoping every day that we would hear," said the doorman. "I haven't said anything to the manager, because he will be as mad as a hornet. He won't be satisfied until he finds out who mixed up the parrots. Then somebody will be fired."

At this moment, Pete, the bellboy, passed the bell captain's desk. He was on his way to the manager's office and he was carrying a special-delivery letter.

The bell captain called to him. "Say, Pete!"

Pete stopped. "Did you call me?" he said.

"Pete!" said the captain. "Did you have something

to do with those parrots the hotel borrowed for the ball?"

"Why . . . ah . . . yes," said Pete. "Willie and I hung them around the ballroom."

"Did anything happen?" said the captain.

"I'm in a hurry now," said Pete. "I have a special-delivery letter here. I have to give it to the manager."

"Give it to me," said the captain. "I'll give it to the manager."

Pete handed the special-delivery letter to the captain.

"Now," said the captain, "tell me what happened to the parrots."

"Well, let me think," said Pete, scratching his head. "Seems to me there were twelve parrots altogether. Or maybe it was thirteen. No, I guess there were eleven."

"Never mind how many there were," said the captain. "What happened to them?"

133

"Oh, they were O.K.!" said Pete. "They seemed to enjoy themselves."

"I don't care whether they enjoyed themselves or not," said the captain. "Did they get out of their cages? That's what I want to know."

"Well . . . ah!" said Pete. "Just a couple of them got out of their cages, but they weren't out very long. Not more than fifteen minutes. Maybe only ten minutes."

"It doesn't make any difference how long they were out of their cages," said the captain. "The important thing is there has been a mix-up and it is all your fault."

"Oh!" said Pete. "A mix-up? That's terrible."

"It *is* terrible!" cried the captain, growing very red in the face. "Bill says some boy is driving him crazy. Says he has the wrong parrot, and we haven't any idea where his parrot is." The captain was growing more and more excited.

"If there was a mix-up," said Pete, "somebody else has a wrong parrot. Have you thought of that?"

"Of course I've thought of it," said the captain.

"Then why haven't they been in to raise the roof?" said Pete.

"I don't know," said the captain. "But just wait until the manager hears about this. Then the roof will be raised."

Just then the telephone on the captain's desk rang. The special-delivery letter was in his hand. He stuck it into his pocket and picked up the receiver. "This is the bell captain," he said. Then he added, "Right away, sir. I'll send a boy up for your bags."

The captain hung up the receiver and turned back to Pete. "Get the bags down from room 193," he said. "They may be the last bags you will carry down. When the manager hears about those parrots, you'll be fired."

"I don't believe they were mixed up," said Pete. "If

they were, the manager would have heard from the people who got the other wrong parrot."

"He will hear!" said the captain, as Pete went off to get the bags. "He will hear!"

But the manager didn't hear. He didn't hear that day or the next day or the next week, because the bell captain had forgotten all about the special-delivery letter that was in his pocket.

CHAPTER 8

EDDIE, THE HUMAN SANDWICH

Eddie had waited and hoped for two weeks for news of Louella. He had heard nothing. He had telephoned to the hotel many times and he had gone to the hotel to inquire for news of his lost parrot. He and the doorman had become very good friends. He now called the doorman Bill.

One afternoon Eddie dropped in to see Bill. There was still no news. As Eddie left the hotel, he saw a man walking by, sandwiched between two signs. As he came toward Eddie, Eddie read *Louis' Shoe Hospital Will Put New Life in Tired Shoes*.

When the man had passed by, Eddie turned to look at the sign on his back. It read *Don't Throw Your Shoes Away. Take Them to Louis*.

Eddie loved signs. He had a big collection of signs, like *Stop! Look! Listen, Low Bridge, Men Working*. The first time he saw a man walking along the street with a sign hanging on his front and another on his back, Eddie had wanted to wear just such signs. Now he suddenly saw that his chance had come.

Eddie ran to the bus stop. He could hardly wait to get home to start making his signs. When he arrived there he rushed into the house. "Hi, Mother!" he shouted.

"I'm upstairs," his mother answered.

Eddie pounded up the stairs. "Mother!" he said. "I want two big pieces of cardboard—big enough to make two signs. Have you got anything?"

"There is a big empty carton in the basement," said his mother. "I just unpacked it."

"Oh, good!" said Eddie. "Am I glad I got in ahead of the twins! They always take the big cartons."

His mother laughed. "Only if you haven't taken them first, Eddie," she said.

Eddie rushed down to the basement, followed by the dog, Reds. The carton was sitting in the center of the floor.

"Oh, boy!" said Eddie, examining the carton. "This is perfect!"

Eddie took his knife out of his pocket. Very carefully, he cut the two large sides out of the carton. Then he went to the shelf where he kept his paints and picked up a large jar of white paint. He leaned his boards against the wall and with a wide brush he covered each board with the white paint. He left them to dry overnight.

When Eddie went to bed, he lay awake for a long time. He was thinking about the signs. He knew what he wanted to say on the signs, but he had a hard time deciding how to say it. Finally he fell asleep.

The next day was Veterans Day, and a holiday. Eddie was in the basement before breakfast. The white paint had dried on the boards. They were ready for the lettering. Eddie got his jar of bright blue paint and a brush. He knew now what he wanted to put on the sign. He had just printed the word *have* when his mother called him to breakfast.

As soon as he finished his breakfast he ran down to the basement, picked up his brush, and set to work again.

He had just finished the word *wrong* when his father called him to come up and help him wash the car. Reds went along. When the car was washed, Eddie returned to his signs. Reds was at his heels.

Eddie had just crossed the *t* in *parrit,* when his mother called him to go to the store. Reds went to the store with Eddie. They ran all the way.

As soon as they were back from the store, Eddie and the dog dashed to the basement. Eddie looked over his work and read it aloud—*Have Wrong Parrit.* He knelt down and started a second line. He hoped he would not be called again, and as quickly as he could he made each letter. When he had finished, the second line read, *Says Old Sourpuss.* Now he was down at the bottom of the board, so he moved over to the second one. At the top he printed *Do You Have My Parrit?*

Just then the twins clattered down the basement stairs like falling rocks.

"Hi, Eddie! What are you doing?" said Frank.

"I'm making a couple of signs," said Eddie.

"What for?" Joe asked.

"To try to get Louella back," replied Eddie.

"How are you going to get Louella back with signs?" said Joe.

"I'm going to wear them," said Eddie. "One on my back and one on my front. Then I'm going to walk up and down in front of the hotel."

"You don't think the person who has Louella is inside the hotel, do you?" asked Frank.

"No," said Eddie.

"Then why are you going to parade up and down outside of the hotel?" said Frank.

"Because it's a good place to walk," said Eddie. "Lots of people will see me."

"How are you going to hitch those signs together?" Frank asked.

"With a couple of straps that I have been saving a long time," said Eddie. "It will work fine."

Eddie went on with his work. He painted the words *Says Eddie Is Best.*

"And how are you going to get these signs down to the hotel?" Frank asked.

"On the bus," Eddie replied.

"You mean you're going to wear that thing on the bus?" exclaimed Joe.

"I'd like to see him sit down in it!" said Frank.

The twins laughed.

"Are you going to wear petticoats under it, Eddie?" said Joe.

This made Eddie mad. As quick as lightning, he lunged toward Frank and painted a streak of blue paint right across his forehead.

Frank and Joe ran upstairs and left Eddie in peace.

The paint on the signs dried quickly. Eddie cut slits

147

near the top of each one. Then he laced the two straps through the slits. He buckled one and left the other loose. Now he was ready to try his signs on. He put the buckled strap over his shoulder and fastened the buckle on the other strap. He walked up and down the basement and was satisfied with the result. Then he took his boards off and carried them upstairs, followed by the dog.

Eddie could hear the twins playing ball in the driveway. He opened the kitchen door and carried his signs outside. Reds went too.

"Hey, Frank!" Eddie called out. "Can you lend me bus fare to get down to the hotel?"

"I haven't any money," replied Frank.

"Joey, can you lend me bus fare?" said Eddie.

"What do you think I am? A millionaire to lend a fellow bus fare?" said Joe.

"You don't have to be a millionaire to lend a fellow bus fare," said Eddie.

"I don't have it," said Joe.

"Well, how am I going to get down to the hotel?" said Eddie.

"Walk," said Frank.

"Sure—walk!" said Joe. "More people will be able to read your signs."

"It's too far to walk," said Eddie. "I wouldn't get back in time for dinner. Maybe not in time for breakfast, even."

Eddie sat down on the stone wall that separated the Wilsons' driveway from the Stewarts' and leaned his signs against the wall. He looked very glum. Reds ran around on the front lawn, sniffing at the bushes.

In a few minutes, Eddie saw Mr. Kilpatrick's red car coming up the street. As Mr. Kilpatrick came nearer, he saw Eddie and waved his hand. He also saw Reds. Mr. Kilpatrick stepped in front of the Wilsons' house. "Hello, Eddie!" he called. "This is a nice dog you have. Have you had him long?"

Eddie went out to the police car. "Well . . . ah," he said, "not very."

"Beautiful dog!" said Mr. Kilpatrick. "Be a terrible thing to lose a dog like that!"

"I guess it would," said Eddie.

"Hear anything about your parrot?" Mr. Kilpatrick asked.

"Not yet," replied Eddie. "But I have a wonderful idea."

"What's the idea?" said Mr. Kilpatrick.

"I'm going to advertise about her," said Eddie.

"In the paper?" asked Mr. Kilpatrick.

"Oh, no! Better than that!" said Eddie. "If you could wait a minute I could show you."

Mr. Kilpatrick looked at his watch. "I can wait a minute," he said.

Eddie ran back to the place where he had left his signs. One had a little more space at the bottom than the other, so he picked it up and carried it back to the basement. He stood it against the wall and opened up the blue paint again. He dipped his brush into the jar and very quickly added a line. It was in rather small letters and it had been done so quickly that it was a little bit hard to read. It said *Also Found Dog—Sorta Red.*

Eddie didn't wait for the paint to dry. He ran back to Mr. Kilpatrick, picking up his other sign on the way.

"Look, Mr. Kilpatrick!" he said, when he reached the car. "See! I'm going to wear these. I'm going to be a sandwich. Everybody will read these signs and I sure hope that whoever has Louella will read them."

Mr. Kilpatrick read the signs. When he got to the very last line he said, "Ho, ho! So you found this dog?"

"Yes, sir!" said Eddie.

"There won't be many people around here to read your signs, Eddie," said the policeman.

"Oh! I'm not going to do it here," said Eddie. "I'm going to walk up and down in front of the hotel, downtown." Then he added, in a doleful voice, "But I can't get there, because I haven't any bus fare."

Mr. Kilpatrick reached across the seat and opened the door of his car. "Get in!" he said. "I'm on my way down there now. I'm on duty at that crossing this afternoon. There is a parade going on."

Eddie yelled to the twins and waved his arms. "Tell Mother I've gone to the parade with Mr. Kilpatrick!" In a moment, Eddie and his signs were in the car and it was heading for the center of the town.

When the twins heard the word *parade,* they gave up their handball game. In no time at all, they had fished enough money for bus fare out of their banks. As they ran down the stairs, Frank called out, "Mother! We're going to see the parade. Eddie's gone with Mr. Kilpatrick."

154

When Eddie reached the hotel, a great many people were lined along the curb. Their faces were all turned the same way—up the street—because they were watching for the parade.

Mr. Kilpatrick parked his car and Eddie got out, with his signs. He soon saw that no one was going to look at him if he walked up and down on the sidewalk. They all had their backs to the sidewalk.

Eddie pushed his way to the edge of the curb and waited. It wasn't long before he heard band music. The parade was coming! Soon he could see the mounted police at the head of the parade. They came nearer and nearer, and the music sounded louder and louder.

The twins got off the bus just in time to see the band go by, led by drum majorettes. After the band came soldiers, then sailors and marines. There were jeeps and tanks and, overhead, army planes.

At the end of the parade there was another band. A

majorette pranced and swung her baton. The bass drum boomed.

Suddenly Frank cried out, "Look, Joey! There's Eddie marching with the band!"

Late that afternoon, when the evening paper came out, it had a picture of Eddie coming and a picture of Eddie going and everyone could read both signs— *Have Wrong Parrit. Says Old Sourpuss. Do You Have My Parrit? Says Eddie Is Best. Also Found Dog— Sorta Red.*

When Eddie's brother Rudy spotted the pictures in the paper, he ran upstairs to Eddie's room to show them to him, but Eddie was sound asleep. He was plumb tuckered out.

CHAPTER 9

THE FAMOUS EDDIE

THE following morning, when Eddie went to school, the boys and girls said, "I saw your picture in the paper, Eddie." Eddie felt quite important. He carried the paper under his arm to show to anyone who had not seen it.

When he showed it to his friend Boodles, Boodles said, "I guess that makes you famous."

"Oh, sure!" said Eddie. "I hope it gets Louella back."

When Anna Patricia arrived, she said, "Eddie, can I have your autograph?"

"Sure! Sure!" said Eddie.

Anna Patricia handed her autograph book to Eddie and he wrote his name on the page. Anna Patricia looked at it and said, "Really, Eddie! I never expected you to be famous!"

Anna Patricia turned to Miss Ross, their teacher, and said, "Miss Ross, did you know that Eddie is famous?" Anna Patricia showed the photograph to Miss Ross. Miss Ross looked at it carefully and said, "That is very nice, but Eddie is not famous for his spelling." Then she said to the class, "Who knows how to spell *parrot?*"

Several hands were raised and Miss Ross asked Sid-

ney to write the word on the blackboard. Sidney wrote it correctly.

Eddie's face turned rather pink. Now he was a famous bad speller, and everyone for miles and miles around knew it.

He didn't worry about it very long. He just hoped that whoever had Louella would see his picture in the paper. He also hoped a little bit that whoever had lost the dog would not see his photograph. Eddie felt somewhat mixed up. He was famous and he was not famous. He hoped one thing would happen and he hoped something else would not.

Later in the week, on Thursday afternoon, a newspaper truck stopped at the Wilsons' house. The boy on the truck jumped out and rang the Wilsons' doorbell. When Rudy opened the door, the driver said, "Does Edward Wilson live here?"

"Yes," replied Rudy.

The parrot was in the living room. "Yawk!" she had screamed when she heard the doorbell. Now she cried out, "Hiya, chum!"

"Is that a parrot?" the boy at the door asked.

"Yes," said Rudy. "She belongs to my brother Eddie. Only she really doesn't. She's the one he got instead of the one he owns, named Louella. We don't know what this one's name is."

"You mean it's sorta mixed up?" said the boy, handing the box to Rudy.

"Sorta is right," said Rudy. "Thanks for the box."

Rudy carried the box into the living room and placed it on a table. Then he called out, "Hey, Eddie! Here's a box just come for you."

Eddie came leaping down the stairs. "A box of what?" he asked.

"I don't know," said Rudy. "It's from the newspaper."

"You don't suppose it's Louella, do you?" said Eddie.

"Nuts!" said Sourpuss.

"In a box!" exclaimed Rudy.

"Well, what else can it be?" Eddie asked.

Just then the twins came in. "What's in the box?" said Frank.

"Eddie thinks it's Louella," said Rudy.

"Louella!" exclaimed Joe. "In a box! Did they kill her?"

"Pickle-push!" cried Sourpuss. "Hit her again."

Eddie's brothers crowded around as he pulled off the string. Eddie could hardly bear to look inside. He held his breath as he lifted the corner of the lid. He expected to see green feathers inside.

Eddie breathed a sigh of relief as he removed the lid. Instead of green feathers, it was filled with letters.

"Yawk!" cried Sourpuss. "Do you like your coffee? How's the coffee?"

No one paid any attention to her. Instead all the boys cried out in a chorus, "Letters!"

Eddie picked up one of the letters. "It has my name on it!" he said.

His brothers picked up more letters from the box. "They all have your name on them," said Rudy.

"Pickle-push!" said Sourpuss. "Nuts!"

"How many do you suppose there are?" said Frank.

"Let's count them," said Joe.

"I want to read them," said Eddie, opening the one in his hand.

He pulled the letter out of the envelope and looked at the handwritten page.

He could read "Dear Eddie." That was as far as he could get. "I can't read this!" he cried. "It looks like somebody just drew mountains."

"Here! Let me see it!" said Rudy. Rudy took the letter out of Eddie's hand and read most of the words.

When he had finished, the boys knew that the person who had written it had lost a red cocker spaniel.

The twins went on counting the letters.

Eddie picked up another one and opened it. This one was easier to read. It had been written on the typewriter, by a boy named Jerry Loomis. He, too, had lost a dog, a dachshund—"sort of red."

Frank was now adding together the number of letters Joe had counted and the number he had counted. "Boy! Oh, boy!" said Frank. "One hundred and nineteen letters! All addressed to Eddie!"

"One hundred and nineteen!" exclaimed Eddie. "What do you suppose they are about? One hundred and nineteen people can't all have Louella. I wish I knew which one tells about Louella. Hurry up! Help me."

The boys set to work ripping open the envelopes but they all found the letters hard to read unless they had been typewritten. So far they all said very much the same thing. All the writers had lost dogs.

"Red dogs must be awfully hard to hold on to," said Rudy. "Everybody loses them."

"But there must be a letter about Louella!" said Eddie.

"Yawk!" cried the parrot. "Old Sourpuss!"

Eddie walked over to the parrot's cage and said, "Look, you! Louella is no sourpuss."

"Nuts!" said the parrot.

"Eddie," said Frank, "it is going to take hours to read all these letters."

When Eddie's father came home, Eddie showed him the box of letters. "Look, Dad!" he said. "Just look at all these letters. They were all written to me, but I can't read most of them."

Mr. Wilson looked over the letters and said, "Never mind. After dinner, I'll help you."

"Thanks, Dad!" said Eddie. "I'm sure there is one there about Louella."

After dinner Eddie and his brothers opened the envelopes, and Mr. Wilson read the letters. Letter after letter was from someone who had lost a dog. Cocker spaniels, collies, setters, Pekinese—all kinds of dogs were lost.

Eddie became more and more impatient. "There must be one from the people who have Louella!" he kept saying.

But when the last letter was read they all knew that there was no letter about Louella.

Eddie looked at the pile of letters and said, "It's all Mr. Kilpatrick's fault. He was the one who wanted me to tell about finding Reds. And now look! All those letters! All about dogs!"

Just then the telephone rang. Mr. Wilson answered it. In a moment he called out, "Eddie! It's for you."

"Who is it?" Eddie called back. "Is it Louella?"

"It doesn't sound like her," said his father.

Eddie ran to the telephone. The family heard him say, "Yes, this is Eddie Wilson. Yes, I got the letters. Thanks."

Then, a few seconds later, they heard him say, "No. There wasn't any about my parrot. They were all from people who had lost dogs." There was a short silence. Then they heard Eddie's voice again. "The dog I found is a golden retriever. There was one letter that said they lost a golden retriever." This was followed by another silence.

Eddie hung up. When he came back from the telephone he said, "That was the newspaper. They wanted to know if any of the letters told about Louella. They said they are going to put the story about me and the letters in the paper tomorrow."

"Eddie!" cried Joe. "A story all about you?"

Sourpuss's cage was covered for the night, but she was not asleep. From under the cover came one word. "Nuts!"

"Eddie, you are getting famouser and famouser all the time," said Frank.

"Pickle-push!" the parrot muttered.

"I don't care how famous I get," said Eddie. "I just want to get Louella back and I don't want to give up Reds."

"I know, Eddie," said his father. "But we'll have to get in touch with that woman who lost a golden retriever."

"I know," said Eddie sadly.

"It's time to go to bed now," said his mother. "It's way past time."

"Do you still think I'll hear about Louella, Mother?" Eddie asked.

"I think you will," his mother replied.

"Good night, Dad," said Eddie.

"Good night, Eddie," his father replied.

Eddie was just getting into bed when he heard the telephone ring again. In a moment it stopped ringing. Eddie knew that someone had answered it. He went into the hall and listened. He could hear his father's voice, but he could not hear what his father was saying.

Eddie went back to his room and climbed into bed. He had just settled himself when his father opened the door and said, "Are you awake, Eddie?"

"Yes, Dad!" Eddie replied.

"Louella is found!" said his father.

Eddie sat up in bed. "Where?" he asked.

"About three hundred miles from here," his father replied.

"Three hundred miles!" exclaimed Eddie. "Did she fly there?"

"No," replied his father. "It's a long story."

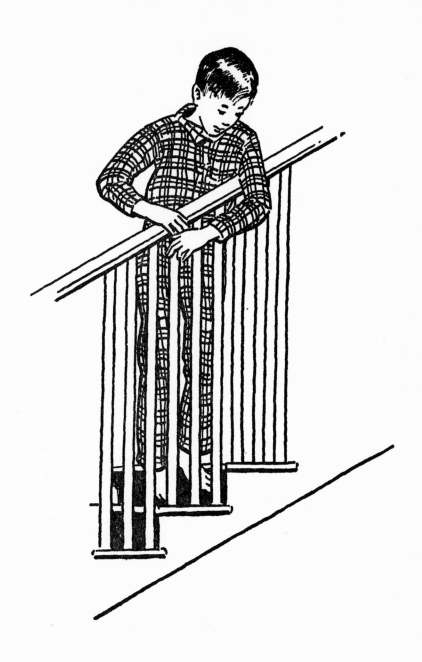

"How did they find out about us?" said Eddie.

"Someone mailed a copy of the paper to them, and they saw your picture," his father replied.

"Well! What do you know!" said Eddie. "How'll we get her?"

"I guess we could drive up over the week end," said his father. "That would be the best way to get this other bird back, too."

"That would be great!" said Eddie.

Mr. Wilson closed the door. In a moment he opened it again. "By the way," he said, "this bird is called Sourpuss."

Eddie laughed and in a moment he was sound asleep.

CHAPTER 10

STRAIGHTENED OUT AT LAST

T HE following morning, Eddie's father made two telephone calls. The first one was a long-distance call to the Tomkinses. Eddie stood beside his father. He didn't want to miss anything.

When Mr. Tomkins answered the telephone, Mr.

Wilson said, "This is Eddie Wilson's father. My son is delighted to know that you have his parrot. The newspaper telephoned late last night."

"He couldn't be happier than my son Tommy is to know that Sourpuss is safe."

Eddie nudged his father. "Ask him if I can speak to Louella," he said.

"Be quiet," said his father.

Eddie waited quietly while his father made plans with Mr. Tomkins to exchange the parrots. Then Eddie nudged his father again. "Can I say hello to Louella?"

"All right, all right," his father replied. Then he said to Mr. Tomkins, "Would it be much trouble for you to bring Louella to the telephone?"

"Who?" said Mr. Tomkins.

"Louella!" Mr. Wilson replied. "The parrot."

"Oh, the parrot!" exclaimed Mr. Tomkins. "Is that

her name?" Then Mr. Tomkins called out, "Tommy, bring the parrot to the telephone." Even Eddie could hear Mr. Tomkins.

"I'll get their parrot," said Eddie. "Maybe they would like to speak to their parrot." Eddie ran into the sun porch and came back with the cage. He stood the cage on the table, close to the telephone.

Mr. Wilson handed the telephone over to Eddie. In a moment Eddie heard Mr. Tomkins's voice. "Here's Louella," he said. "She's right here."

"Hello, Louella!" Eddie shouted eagerly into the telephone.

Louella made no reply.

"Hello, Louella!" Eddie shouted again. "Who's best, Louella?"

"Old Sourpuss," said Louella, to Eddie's great surprise.

Eddie tried hard to get Louella to say something else,

but she remained silent. Finally Eddie said, "Here's Sourpuss. Do you want to talk to her?"

"Sure!" said a boy's voice. "This is Tommy."

Eddie held the receiver up to the parrot's cage and he heard Tommy shout, "Hello, Sourpuss! Do you know who this is, Sourpuss?"

"Nuts!" said Sourpuss.

"What did she say?" said Tommy.

"She said 'Nuts'!" said Eddie.

"That's Sourpuss, all right," said Tommy.

"So long!" said Eddie. "I'll see you tomorrow."

"So long!" said Tommy.

The next telephone call that Mr. Wilson made was to Mrs. Pinny, the woman who had sent a letter saying that she had lost a golden retriever. Eddie felt uneasy now as he stood beside his father. He didn't want to give up Reds.

The woman on the other end of the telephone spoke

179

in a very loud voice. "Oh, yes!" she shouted. "I'll come tomorrow morning to see my dog. I am sure you have my dog. He will know me at once. I'll be so glad to get my Bossie back." Eddie could hear her plainly.

"Be sure to come before nine o'clock," said Eddie's father. "We have to take a long drive tomorrow."

"I'll be there!" shouted Mrs. Pinny.

"Bossie!" cried Eddie, as his father hung up the receiver. "Whoever heard of calling a dog Bossie? That's a name for a cow."

The following morning, Eddie and his father were up early. Mrs. Wilson packed a bag with the clothes they would need for their overnight trip. She also packed some sandwiches for their lunch.

Meanwhile, Eddie cleaned Sourpuss's cage. He wanted the Tomkinses to see that he had taken good care of their bird.

Reds kept running around, and every once in a while

he would bark. He seemed to know that something was going on.

No one was cheerful at breakfast. Everyone felt jumpy and they all knew it was because of Reds. All the Wilsons loved Reds and now, in the next hour, they might lose him. A strange woman was coming and she might take Reds away.

Eddie's father looked at Reds and said, "I can't believe that dog's name is Bossie."

"Here, Bossie! Here, Bossie!" Rudy called out. Reds looked at Rudy with a puzzled expression.

"He looks as though he was going to be sick," said Frank.

"You would be sick too, if your name was Bossie," said Joe.

"We'll soon know," said Mr. Wilson. "If Reds belongs to Mrs. Pinny, he'll know her at once. It all depends on how Reds behaves when she arrives."

"I hope Reds bites her," said Eddie.

"Oh, Eddie!" exclaimed his mother. "What a terrible thing to say! You know you don't mean that."

Eddie hung his head and said, "Well, I don't mean *bite* her. I just mean *taste* her."

"Oh, no, Eddie!" Frank cried. "That would mean he would lick her, and Reds just licks the people he likes."

"Oh!" sighed Eddie, as he finished his breakfast. "I just wish she would come."

Eddie decided to put the parrot in the car. Then they could leave at once, when the matter of the dog was settled. He opened the front door and Reds ran outside, followed by Eddie, who walked out with the cage in his hand.

At that very moment Eddie saw a car stop in front of the house. Then a very large lady stepped out. He guessed that this was Mrs. Pinny.

As soon as she saw Reds, she threw her arms out wide and cried, "Oh, my Bossie! Bossie!"

"Yawk!" screamed Sourpuss. "Nuts!"

Reds turned toward Mrs. Pinny and began to bark furiously.

"Oh, Bossie!" said Mrs. Pinny, walking toward Reds. "Don't you know me? Don't you know Tootsie?"

"Yawk!" yelled Sourpuss. "Nuts!"

"Gr-r-r-r-r!" growled Reds.

"Oh!" said Mrs. Pinny. "This is a very vicious dog. My Bossie was a gentle dog."

"Oh yes!" said Eddie. "I guess this isn't your dog at all."

"No," said Mrs. Pinny. "My Bossie was a gentle dog."

Eddie placed the parrot's cage on the stone wall and ran out to Mrs. Pinny's car. As she stepped into the car, Eddie said, "I hope you find your dog."

"Thank you," said Mrs. Pinny. "I hope I do. It's too bad you have such a vicious dog!"

"Oh, we don't mind," said Eddie. "We're used to him."

Eddie's brothers were looking out of the upstairs windows. As soon as the car drove away, they threw open the windows and shouted to Eddie.

Eddie was jumping up and down, yelling, "He wasn't her dog. He wasn't her dog."

"Hey, Eddie! What did she say?" Joe called out.

"She said he was vicious," Eddie called back.

"Nuts!" shouted Sourpuss. "Nuts!"

"Nuts is right," said Frank.

Eddie and his father were off in a few minutes. They both felt happy now. Sourpuss was on the seat beside Eddie. Her cage was covered with a cloth, for the trip. Sourpuss didn't like to be covered, so she muttered to herself. Reds went along on the back seat.

It was a long drive. At noon Eddie and his father ate their sandwiches. Late in the afternoon, they drove into the Tomkinses' driveway.

Tommy had been watching for the Wilsons' car for a long time. Now he ran out, calling, "Hello! Hello! Where's old Sourpuss?"

Eddie jumped out of the car and said, "Hi, Tommy! Here she is." He handed the cage to Tommy, and Tommy lifted the cover. Tommy's face was one big smile. "Hello, Sourpuss!" he said.

"Hiyah, pal!" said Sourpuss.

"Come on in," said Tommy, to Eddie and his father. "I guess Louella will be awfully glad to see you."

"I hope you don't mind our bringing Reds," said Eddie. "Reds is our golden retriever." Reds jumped out as Eddie opened the back door.

"Oh, he's a nice dog," said Tommy. "Is this the dog you found?"

"Yes," said Eddie, "but he's ours now. Nobody claimed him."

Tommy led the way into the house, and Eddie and his father were welcomed by Mr. and Mrs. Tomkins.

Tommy led Eddie right to Louella's cage. "Yawk!" cried Louella.

"Hello, Louella!" said Eddie. "You know me, don't you, Louella?"

Louella closed her eyes.

"Louella!" said Eddie. "It's me, Louella!"

Louella just sat with her eyes closed.

"Oh, Dad!" Eddie called to his father. "Louella is mad. She won't open her eyes."

"Well, she can't keep them closed forever," said his father. "Don't pay any attention to her."

"That's hard to do," said Eddie, " 'cause I'm so glad to see her. But she isn't glad to see me."

"Maybe this isn't Louella after all," said Tommy.

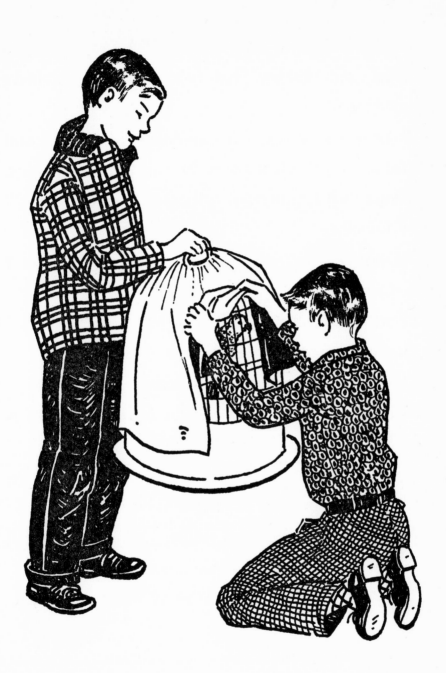

"She looks like Louella," said Eddie.

"So does Sourpuss look like Louella," said Tommy.

Eddie looked very worried. After all, Reds had looked like Mrs. Pinny's Bossie, but Reds wasn't Bossie.

Eddie turned away from the cage. Just as he was walking out of the room, Louella opened her eyes and yelled, "Yawk! Yawk! Eddie is best!"

Eddie turned and ran back to the cage. "Oh! It's Louella, all right. It's Louella!"

Eddie and his father spent the night with the Tomkinses. Tommy and Eddie had a lot to talk about. By the time Mr. Wilson and Eddie left the following morning, they were all good friends.

As Eddie carried Louella's cage out to the car, Reds ran beside Eddie. "Yawk!" cried Louella. "Cats!"

"Now Louella!" said Eddie. "This is Reds. He is our nice dog. He is the nicest dog we ever had."

Louella didn't care how nice Reds was. She sat on the

front seat of the car beside Eddie. All the way home, every time Reds moved in the back of the car, Louella said from under the cover, "Cats! Cats!"

DATE DUE

GAYLORD			PRINTED IN U.S.A